WHISKEY THRENODY 2

Christmas In The Mountains

Daniel Elijah Sanderfer

Mountain Ranch Publishing

Cover design by: Daniel Elijah Sanderfer
Printed in the United States of America

To Steve at Look Twice in Pennington Gap, Virginia. Thank you for reminding me that we exist. We've always existed. Thank you for being a friend.

WHISKEY THRENODY 2

CHRISTMAS IN THE MOUNTAINS

DANIEL ELIJAH SANDERFER

PART ONE

EMMETT

The wind bustled outside, kicking up a whirlwind of leaves as it did. A few wayward snowflakes fell onto the windowsill outside. The sound of mom coming down the stairs momentarily distracted me before I turned my gaze back outside. I sighed as I continued anxiously staring out toward the dirt road that leads to the farmhouse. She sat a box of Christmas decorations on the coffee table. "The weatherman says there's a chance for snow here in the mountains tonight."

"Really," I gushed.

Mom nodded. "Wouldn't that be a great way to kick off our first Christmas back in the mountains?"

"Uh-huh," I mumbled as I propped my fist under my chin.

"Aw," mom sighed as she came up behind me and wrapped her arms around my body. "Don't worry, Emmett, Robert Lee will be back from hunting with his dad soon."

The sound of a vehicle coming down the road prompted me to perk up a little. A little rusted-out red pickup truck with farm use tags turned onto the dirt road. I began to dance around and shout, "It's him, It's him, he's back!"

Mom giggled and made a path to the door. "Calm down, Mary! You're gonna knock something over and break it."

I barely heard what she said as I threw on my flannel shirt and bolted out the door. I emerged onto the porch just as Robert Lee got out of the pickup. He flashed me a wicked smile that made me die a little inside. He was carrying a grocery bag as he sauntered in my direction. I couldn't contain myself any longer and bolted from the porch like a streak of lightning.

He was still wearing his camo pants and hunting vest. He knows how hot that makes me. He sat the bag and braced himself as I dove into his arms and buried my face in his chest. "I missed you so much!"

"I missed you too," he replied with his standard low growl. Ever since we met, it seems as if we've been living in a fairytale. He comes to see me every day after completing his chores, and we walk and spend time together. When you last heard from us, it was Autumn, and we'd taken to camping on the land here around Grandpa and Grandma's old farm. Although it hadn't seen a plow or cow in years, it was still full of life and wonder.

I was looking forward to our first Christmas together and still am. Thanksgiving was a somewhat subdued affair. Robert Lee ate dinner with his folks around noon. Then he came over here for more dinner. That boy can eat, and I love watching him eat. He can put down a couple of plates and not even blink. Then, still want dessert. Mom says he's a growing boy, and that's the way country boys eat. If I ate that much, I'd be in a food coma for days and not be able to move.

Mom says hard-working boys like him need their energy. I like to see him happy. I like to see him enjoying things. Especially when it's food I helped prepare. Mama says I've got a country girl's heart, and one day all that heavy food will catch up to him. Then, he'll be one of those cute big ole' red-neck guys we see in town. Right now, I don't want to think about getting older. I want to live forever in this fairytale world with my sexy knight in shining Under Armour.

As we separated, he pecked my cheek and made me blush. I always do when he holds me with one arm and kisses me. "What's in the bag?"

“A deer roast for your mom. Mama sent it over.”

“Well, she'll definitely enjoy that.”

We started toward the porch, and he held the front door open as we stepped inside. Mom was busy rooting through the box she brought down as she turned to greet us. “Howdy, Robert Lee. How was the hunting today?”

“Daddy shot a six-pointer, and I helped clean it. By the way, mama sent this over.”

She peeked inside. “Mmm, deer roast, my favor-ite! I'll put this in the crockpot tonight, and it can be lunch tomorrow.”

She disappeared around the corner to put it in the fridge and remerged, drying her hands. “Robert Lee, while you're here, why don't you and Emmett go down into the woods and find us a tree?”

“Yes, ma'am,” he said respectfully as we stepped back outside. We turned the corner of the house and made our way to the woodshed. He knows where everything is pretty well now and went right for the ax. Silently, we started down the footpath that ventured deeper into the woods. I latched on to Robert Lee's arm and snuggled up closer to him as we walked along. "Have you thought about what you're getting your folks for Christmas?"

His eyes were searching the forest as he replied, "I'll probably just get mama some of her Charlie perfume from the drug store, and she'll probably grab a pack of beer and put my name on it for dad."

"What about me?"

A clever glint flashed in his eye, "Nice try."

I stopped him and protested. "Come on!"

His expression turned stern. "I told ya, I ain't gonna say. It's a surprise!"

I pouted, and we continued onward down the trail. In my mind, I knew he wasn't going to tell me. I just like messing with him. "Just a hint," I added.

"Nope!"

ROBERT LEE

The truth is that I honestly don't know what to get Emmett yet. We've known each other for almost a year now. I know he likes flannel shirts, but that seems kind of impersonal. Most boys buy their girls perfume or makeup, but I don't know what he wears. All I know is he always smells so good when he gets close to me.

Mama said we'd go up to Lee County and shop in Pennington this weekend. I'm hoping I can find something there for him. In the meantime, I just gotta keep him distracted. This Christmas is a big deal. Before we met, I never had to worry about buying something for anyone but my folks. Now, I feel all this responsibility to find him something perfect. Something that he'll love and cherish for the rest of his life.

While I was lost in my thoughts, Emmett rushed ahead and circled a large spruce in the middle of a clearing. His eyes were lit-up with child-like wonder as he turned to me. "Can we get this one?"

I gave it a once-over and decided to give him a little show. "No problem," I growled as I approached the tree and tried to assess how to cut it. I'm a tall boy, but this thing was probably tinkering on the better side of eight feet. "Stand back," I said as I poised the ax. It didn't take too long before I called out, "Timber," and watched it collapse.

Emmett ran to me when it was down and playfully punched my arm. "So strong. That's my man!"

I tried to play it cool and muttered, "It was nothing at all," before scooping him into my arm and bringing his body close to mine. His eyes spun around in wonder as he blushed and looked away. "Robert Lee, we better hurry and get the tree home before it gets dark."

He poised his hands on my chest and tried to push away, but I just tightened my grip around his waist. "Don't be in such a hurry. We haven't seen each other all day."

His eyes found their way back to mine, and he

smiled. “I know, but there will be plenty of time for fooling around later.”

I rolled my eyes and reluctantly accepted a kiss before making my way to the trunk. “Now, I have a reason to get it back. You grab the top, and I’ll grab the bottom.”

Happily, we marched along the path from which we came. When we got back to his house, his mom spotted us from the door and rushed to open it. “My goodness, you boys are strong. It’s a good thing I found that tree stand while you were gone.”

“Where would you like it,” I grunted as I tried to get a better grip.

“Right in front of the window.”

After a minor struggle, Emmett and I managed to get it upright and secured in the stand before stepping back. “Oh, it’s beautiful,” his mom gushed. Emmett just stood there gazing upon it in silent wonder as a smile formed on my lips. After a brief pause of admiration, his mom interrupted the silence. “I hate to ask but would you boy mind grabbing a few pieces of wood to get us through the night.”

“Sure,” I said as Emmett groaned. “It won’t be so bad,” I added as I grabbed his shoulders and pushed him back outside.

His mom just giggled and buried her hands inside a box of old-fashioned lights with the screw-on bulbs. On the way to the woodshed, Emmett rushed ahead and disappeared behind the door. I stepped inside to find him leaning against the wall.

"The one good thing about coming back outside is maybe we can pick up where you left off out in the woods."

I bit my bottom lip and approached. Being a boy of a certain age, I wasn't about to turn down any kind of action he was willing to toss my way. I poised my hand on the wall above him and leaned in. "Come here often?"

He leaned in and hummed, "Not nearly as often as I would like."

I started with a kiss. One that he basked in the longer I held it. I could feel his fingers digging into my shoulder as soft moans vibrated from his nose. I love it when he hangs on to me. My camo pants were getting tighter by the second. His hand found my knob and began to massage. The sensation was enough to make me release his lips and sigh. "Oh, yeah."

"You like that?"

"Hell yeah," I whispered.

"How about if I just unzip these?"

I felt my zipper slide down. Then my pants come unbuttoned. I shuttered at the feeling of his hand slipping into my boxer briefs. He was rubbing and stroking away as we stole hard passionate kisses. It may be cold outside, but it was hot as hell in this woodshed. Before long, I felt myself getting close. At the time, I was munching on his neck, and he was whimpering, "Oh, yes," in my ear.

My statement came in the form of a muffled growl, "I'm gonna blow."

"Give it to me," he hissed.

His pace quickened. My muscles tensed. I couldn't hold back anymore. Just before I blew my load, he fell to his knees and wrapped his lips tightly around my swollen member. My face washed with shock and amazement. He took it all as I stood there, letting my gun fire off shot after shot right into his sweet mouth.

Then, when it was all over, he stood and wiped his lips on his shirt sleeve. For a moment, I just stood there with my exposed cock, trying to catch my breath as he turned to grab a few pieces of wood. "Aren't you going to get some wood?"

"I already did," I exhaled as he giggled and ran off back to the house.

Hurriedly, I tucked myself away then zipped up before snagging a few pieces and running to catch up with him. A smile formed on my lips. He never ceases to amaze me. On the outside, he seems like such a quiet and well-mannered boy. But behind closed doors, he's a vixen of sorts. It's one of the things that drives me wild about him.

Back inside the house, Emmett neatly stacked his wood into a carrier on the hearth. I followed his lead and turned to find his mom stringing lights. "Here," I offered, "I'll do that!"

She stepped back, "Why, thank you, Robert Lee."

"I'll help too," Emmett chimed in.

His mom just stood back. "Well, if you boys have it under control, I'll just go see if those cookies are ready."

"Cookies," Emmett shouted. "You mean Grandma's Christmas Cookies?"

"Yep," she giggled.

"I thought she was the only one who knew how to make them and refused to give anyone the recipe."

His mom called back from around the corner. "She did. However, I found it written on a card in her recipe box."

"Alright," he cheered as he turned his focus back to me.

I'd finished stringing the lights while he was talking to her. "Grandma's cookies are the best! She used to mail them to us every year before we came back to the mountains."

"They sound delicious. Of course, I'm usually up for dessert any time of day."

Emmett grinned as I grabbed the garland and started draping it over the tree's branches. His eyes twinkled. "I've already had something to eat, but there's always room for cookies."

I smirked and shushed him as he wiggled his eyebrows. A moment later, his mom emerged from around the corner with a festive plate of white cookies topped with sprinkles and sugar. Emmett took one, as did I, and we simultaneously bit down. His mom was a second behind, and we all sighed with content.

I finished mine first, then wiped my hands on my pants legs. "I hate to eat and run, but I better get back home before dinner. Mama will be upset if I'm late."

Emmett frowned. "Do you have to?"

"Fraid so."

"Okay," he sighed.

I made my way for the door as his mom thanked me for all the help. He rushed to finish his cookie, then followed me out to the truck like a sad puppy. "What time will you be by tomorrow?"

I rubbed the back of my neck, "I'm not sure. I have to go shopping with mama. Then daddy wants to try and get one more deer to put in the freezer."

"Please be careful," Emmett added as he met my gaze.

I opened my arms to wrap him in a hug, and he forcefully dove into me. "Won't it be nice when we don't have to say goodbye every day?"

"It sure will," I whispered as I stroked his back. Yet inside, my mind was plagued with thoughts of what to get him. We separated, and I gave him another kiss before climbing into the truck and speeding off down his driveway. In the rearview mirror, I could still see him waving when I turned onto the little one-lane road that leads to home. That is always the part that breaks my heart the most.

I told myself to stop looking, but my eyes always seem to find him, and I can't look away. It's the way it goes every time I'm with him. I just love him so freaking much that he grabs all of my attention. When I came to the intersection of Ms. Savannah's country store, I decided to stop in and grab myself an

RC and a candy bar.

She was busy sweeping the snow off the porch when I got out. "Howdy, Robert Lee! You been off to see Emmett Ray?"

"Yes, ma'am."

"Have you bought him something nice for Christmas yet?"

"No," I groaned. "I've been racking my brains trying to figure out what to get him.

Ms. Savannah shook her head. "Well, don't fret none. I'm sure something will come to ya soon."

She followed me inside as I grabbed a cold one from the cooler and sat it on top of the counter. While she was ringing it up, I set the candy bar up there too. It's no secret that Emmett Ray and I are an item now in this small town. Some folks look at us with disgust and judgmental eyes. But Ms. Savannah doesn't mind one bit. She said back in the day; she used to hang out with all kinds of boys that liked boys at a party house back in the woods. She said that back then, people didn't pay much attention to folks the way they do now

I wish it were still that way. Don't get me wrong, she told me they had their own struggles, but out there, people congregated to smoke, drink, and listen to records. My folks don't care much for music. Every once in a while, mama used to put on her cassette of Tammy Wynette's Greatest Hits, but other than that, they didn't believe much in secular music. The reverend at the church always preached that secular music was a gateway to hell.

I know every time I get in the pickup, I turn the radio on and get lost in the tunes. Maybe when Emmett and I get a place of our own we can have a record player or something. I've always dreamed of slow dancin' with him. After paying for my soda and candy bar, I got back in the truck and crossed the road to go home. The pickup bounced and bobbed with the ruts of the graveled road. Daddy's hunting dogs ran alongside and barked with glee when I turned up the driveway.

I could see daddy out in the pasture tending to one of the cows when I got out. Despite our humble life, I know I wouldn't want to be anywhere else. There ain't nothin' I need as long as I got Emmett. As I stepped inside, Mama shouted from around the corner, "Robert, Robert Lee, is that you?"

"Yes, ma'am."

I followed her voice and emerged in the doorway of the kitchen. "How was Emmett?"

"Good, his mom had us help her get a tree and set it up."

"That's nice. I just wanted to remind you to make sure you get plenty of rest tonight. It's a long ride over the mountain to Lee County. Then we still have to drive over from Jonesville to Pennington."

"I will."

"Dinner will be ready soon, so go wash up."

"What are we having?"

"I fixed a roast from the deer you and daddy got earlier."

"Awesome."

She turned around and met my gaze with a smile. "Do you know what you're getting Emmett Ray for Christmas yet?"

"Not yet," I sighed. "I guess I'll know when I see it."

She approached and patted my cheek. "Don't worry. I'm sure he'll love anything you pick out. Besides, Christmas ain't about the gifts. It's about spending time with the ones you love."

I smiled big as she continued. "Now, don't forget, while we're up in Lee County, I want to stop by and visit your Aunt Lou."

"Ugh," I groaned, "That's means I'll have to visit with Cousin Darcy and all her sisters. Can't I just come home and let you and daddy see them."

"No, you know how much your Aunt Lou loves you, and so do her girls."

"But they always try to lure me out to the barn and try to kiss me."

Mama looked stern for a moment. "Oh, they're just teasing."

"They are not. The last time we were there, Cousin Darcy tried to show me her underwear."

"Robert Lee!"

I bowed my head. "You know better than to be tellin' stories right here at Christmas."

"But it ain't a story, Mama."

She remained silent for a moment before speaking again. "Well, if they make you that uncomfortable, then just stay inside with daddy and me."

"Okay."

"Now go get washed up."

"Yes, ma'am."

The thought of seeing my cousins again wasn't a very nice thought. It's eating Aunt Lou alive that I found a beau before Darcy Lynn. Maybe if she didn't look like a horse, she'd have already roped a guy. I snickered at the thought of offering her a carrot, but mama would kill me.

Anyways, I wish she hadn't have sprung this bit of news on me. I have enough on my mind trying to figure out the perfect gift for Emmett. I closed my eyes as I washed my hands. Sweet Emmett. Never in this world did I think the boy of my dreams would show up out here. He drives me wild, wild, I tell ya. So much so that he's all I think about day and night. He deserves the best of everything, and I swear to God I'll work till my dying day to make sure he has everything his heart desires.

I finished washing my hands and dried them on a towel before stepping back into the hallway. Daddy was just getting in and nodded a greeting my way. "Did you wash up, Robert Lee?"

"Yes, sir."

"Dinner ready?"

"Mm-hmm."

"Do you got a minute?"

"Yeah."

He opened the door, and we stepped outside. He seemed kind of anxious as he led the way to the barn. Inside, he had something covered with an old tarp. He pulled it away to reveal a brand-new hand-made rocking chair. “You think your mama will like it?”

I walked around it with a grin. “Oh, Daddy, she’ll love it! When’d you have the time to build it?”

“I just worked on it in the evenings, in between tending to the animals and land.”

“Well, she’ll absolutely love it.”

“Good,” he exhaled. “I know her other one was getting quite worn. Hell, I’ve done put the rockers back on it a hundred times this past year.”

I smiled and replied with a quiet tone, “Trust me, she’ll love it.”

“Good,” he said as he covered it back up and turned his attention to me.

I was lost staring pensively at the covered chair. “What’s the matter with you, boy?”

I shook my head. “Nothin’ daddy. I’m just worried about what to get Emmett Ray.”

“Well,” he cleared his throat. “I ain’t sure what boys like, but the first Christmas with your mama, I got her a scarf and some perfume.”

“See, that’s the thing,” I sat down, “I don’t think Emmett wears any cologne or anything.”

Daddy propped his leg on a nearby stool, “Well, what does he like?”

“I know he likes cookies and food.”

“Well, don’t we all,” he chuckled.

“Right,” I smirked. “Other than that, I don’t really know.”

The sound of mama’s voice echoed through the hollow. “Russell? Robert Lee? Suppers on the table!”

Daddy cut his eyes then turned them back to me. "I'm sure you'll figure out something, son."

"Yeah," I sighed as I stood and followed daddy out of the barn.

"What were y'all up to?"

Daddy met mama's gaze. "The boy and I were just talking."

"Oh, okay. As I said, Suppers ready, so quit fiddlefarting around and get in here before it gets cold."

The roast was delicious, as expected. Dinner, however, was a quiet affair. Mama, of course, told Daddy about the happenings of the day and the latest gossip in the hollow. She'd get a bath tonight and get gussied up for our trip to town. Usually, she just washes up in the old pitcher and bowl in her bedroom and only washes her hair once a week. If it's cold out, she'll wear a kerchief and make me wear a hat. She's still very old-fashioned that way.

When dinner was finished, I retired to my room to think more about what to get for Emmett. It'd be nice to get out of town, even if it was just over the mountain to Lee County.

PART TWO

ROBERT LEE

In the morning, the old alarm clock by my bed rang out like a songbird. Mama had told me to be up at sunrise so we could load up the gifts she'd made for my cousins and aunt. I could already hear the pickup running outside. Daddy usually had to warm it up before we drove it anywhere because the heater didn't work too well.

I was sitting on the side of the bed trying to get awake when mama knocked. "Robert Lee, are you up? We need to get going!"

"Yes, ma'am."

I stood and hurried to put on my Sunday best; a nice pair of slacks, a button-up shirt tucked in, and a red sweater. Mama was a stickler about dressing up to go to town. Even though we don't have much money, she said the Lord wanted us to look our best when out amongst people. She always frowns when she sees people with their shirts off at the gas station or kids running around barefoot in a store.

Although Jonesville is a little town like ours, it has a different vibe. The farmers and people up there make good money. We only go up there during

Christmas and Easter to visit relations and Walmart. Daddy refuses to go in. He says places like Walmart are destroying America's small businesses and taking money away from working families. Personally, I feel like they do good by giving jobs to all those people who usually wouldn't be able to find work in town.

I mean, all there is in Lee County are farms and mountains. One of the things I like the most about going up there is seeing the mountains stretch out far and wide along the horizon. Also, there are lots of cows. I like cows. I think no matter how old I get, every time I pass a herd of cows on the side of the road, I have to point them out. Mama and Daddy always just smile and say, "Yep."

I was finally dressed and stepped out of my bedroom just as mom passed by with her purse. "You ready to go?"

"Yes, ma'am," I mumbled with a sleepy tone.

"Well, Daddy is already in the truck and waiting on us."

"Did he load up the presents for Aunt Lou's family?"

"Yes."

We filed down the stairs, and mama did one last check to make sure all the lights were off. I stepped onto the porch and took a breath of the frosty air as mama closed the door behind us. She held my arms as she followed the steps down, then I opened the truck door for her. Thankfully, Daddy decided to take the extended cab today, so I wouldn't have to ride in the bed all the way over the mountain. Once we were all inside and buckled in, Daddy shifted into gear and backed out of the driveway.

EMMETT

I hate when Robert Lee goes away. Especially far away, like Lee County. It's like forty minutes from here. Mom and I woke up earlier and picked up where we left off last night. I'd gotten momentarily lost in my thoughts while hanging an ornament on the tree when mom's voice broke the silence. "Hey, that's looking great!"

"Thanks," I mumbled.

"I never have the patience to hang all those ornaments with changing their positions a thousand times."

"That's because you have P.O.P.D."

"What the heck is that?"

"Perfect ornament placement disorder," I grinned.

Mom chuckled, "You're not right."

"The trick to decorating a tree is letting the ornament tell you where it wants to be, then voila!"

I hung another ornament and smiled at her. Mom just pursed her lips and quipped, "show off," before grabbing some empty Christmas storage boxes and heading upstairs. It would undoubtedly be a long day without seeing Robert Lee, but I know he's with his folks Christmas shopping. Every time he goes out to hunt with his dad, all these horrible scenarios play through my head. What if he gets shot by another hunter? What if they run into a bear? What if something happens to the truck where they can't get home?

I shook my head to snap myself out of the bad dream currently playing in my mind. No, I wouldn't worry today. Today I would just hang out with mom and decorate the house. I've already bought his present, and I know he's going to love it. However, something has been bothering me since last night. I hope I didn't put too much pressure on him to find me the perfect gift. The last thing I want my boyfriend to be is stressed at Christmas. In all honesty, he is my present. He doesn't have to get me anything at all. Just being here is a gift in itself. I just wished I'd have told him that last night.

ROBERT LEE

Dad pulled into a spot right outside the Westgate Mini Mall in Pennington Gap, Virginia. The storefronts were decorated with humble displays and dawned sale signs. Mama hopped out and made a b-line for the Rise and Shine Spa while I lingered momentarily by the door of the truck. "Aren't you going in with your mom?"

I met dad's gaze. "In there?"

"Yeah."

"Nah, it's full of girly stuff and smells funny."

Dad chuckled. "Well, if you don't want to go in there, why don't you check out that little shop next door? They might have something you can get for Emmett."

"Okay."

I finally closed the truck door and tucked my hands into my pockets. Going into stores by myself always makes me nervous. I always feel like they're going to think I'm a thief or something. Then, I don't know what to do with my hands once inside. I feel like if I leave them in my pockets, the shop owner will think I'm up to something, or worse yet, that I've pocketed something.

Regardless of those fears, Walmart didn't have anything suitable for my boy. So, I guess it's here or bust. After this, we've got to visit Aunt Lou and my cousins. I stepped inside to the smell of scented wax and eucalyptus. It was a pleasant and welcoming smell. An older woman took her bag from the guy running the register and wished him a Merry Christmas before passing me and heading outside. I browsed several shelves filled with porcelain bears and attractive primitive décor.

Up on the walls were large canvases painted with barnyard and mountain scenes. A funny smile formed on my lips as I thought about what Emmett and my house would look like when we get older. I think I'd like some paintings like that inside. They remind me so much of the hollow where we live.

The man at the register stepped around the counter and daintily straightened up a few misconstrued items before smiling at me. "Can I help you?"

"Um," I mumbled. "I'm just browsing, but thanks."

He smiled again, "Well, if you need anything at all, don't hesitate to ask. That's what we're here for."

Silence lingered for a moment as I cast my eyes over a booth filled with dishes and kitchen décor. I didn't need anything like that, so I carried on while the shop owner carried on with his tidying. "Is it something for a girl?"

"Huh?"

I turned to him as he continued. "The present you're looking for, might it be for a girlfriend?"

"Not exactly," my face turned red.

"A family member?"

"No, sir."

Something about his sweet and charming demeanor made me feel safe. It was a safety I only felt around people like me… such as Emmett. The brief thought that he might be a member of the family so to say, crossed my mind. Still, I managed to find the courage to whisper, "Actually, it's for my boyfriend."

"Oh!" The man's smile turned into a grin. "Well, I can definitely help you with that."

He winked, "My name is Steve, by the way."

"Robert Lee," I replied as I extended my hand.

"Robert Lee," the man shook his head with a warm expression. "You can't meet a guy around here that doesn't have two names." He pointed to himself, "I'm Stevie Ray, and my sister is Patricia May."

"Hey," I interrupted, "My boyfriend's name is Emmett Ray."

"Well, how about that?"

He led me to the back of the store to a wall filled with beautiful pictures and trinkets from the sea. "My boyfriend, sorry, husband was in the Navy. We traveled all around before he... before he um passed."

I bowed my head, "I'm sorry."

"Don't be," Steve waved. "We had a wonderful life, and I cherish the memories we shared. Just as I'm sure you will with your Emmett."

He picked up a lighthouse and flicked a switch. From the bottom, the sound of seagulls and ocean waves echoed throughout the room. "Wow," I exhaled, "that's beautiful."

"Yes," Steve replied warmly. "Maybe something like this would be a nice gift for your beau."

"But what's so special about a lighthouse?"

"Well," Steve began, "Lighthouses are a symbol of strength. They are a beacon of hope guiding wayward and lost sailor's home. They can withstand the strongest storms and provide shelter to keep the sea birds warm. They are so much more than just a building. They are a symbol of hope. A guiding light reassuring you that no matter how lost or alone you feel, there's something always there to guide you home.

I think the same applies when we fall in love. We become a lighthouse in that person's life. We become a beacon on the days where they might not be able to see the light. They, in turn, do the same for us when we're in the dark. Love is like the ocean, ever-changing. Sometimes the waters are turbulent.

Sometimes they are calm. But even when the storms come and toss up the waves, the lighthouse is always there to guide us safely home. So be his lighthouse, Robert Lee. Be his shelter in the storm. Be the one he goes to when his sails are tattered and torn. I promise that in time, you will find all the love and warmth you provide will come back a hundredfold."

I sniffled and wiped my eyes. It was the perfect gift with the perfect meaning. Although Emmett Ray and me have only been together for a short time, I know that he's the one I'm going to spend the rest of my life with. Steve and I watched the little light at the top of the porcelain lighthouse continue to turn for a moment longer before I managed to say, "I'll take it."

Steve proudly carried it to the front of the store and started wrapping it. "Will there be anything else?"

I scanned the store again. "I think I will take one more look around before I go. I think I missed some stuff on the first go around."

"And that's why we're called Look Twice," Steve added as he bagged my lighthouse.

In my mind, I couldn't help but think about what a charming place this was. Also, the fact that someone else like me existed in this backwoods place. I go back to the times where I felt so different and alone. Like I was the only gay boy in this whole state. But meeting someone like Emmett and now Steve confirmed that we exist, that we've always existed. That there isn't anything abnormal or wrong with me. For the first time, I felt affirmed. I'm a proud gay man. I always have been, and I always will be.

Pleased with my present, I returned to the truck around the same time mama did. She glanced at the gift bag I was carrying and smiled, "Aw, I take it you found what you were looking for?"

"Yes, ma'am."

"Well, we best be getting to Aunt Lou's."

We piled into the truck and drove away from town. Aunt Lou lives at the top of a mountain in the nearby town of Hurricane. The homes on top of the ridge are humble and surrounded by farms. At one time, Aunt Lou and Uncle Lester owned about fifty acres. However, they sold a piece here and there as they needed money. Now they own about ten acres right around the house. My mind drifted to Emmett as we started up the one-lane road. I wished I was going home to see him instead of forcing myself to make small talk with kin.

As we pulled into the dirt road that led to the ranch, daddy got out to open the pasture gate. A bumpy quarter of a mile later, the house came into view. There were old appliances and a couch on the front porch. A group of Uncle Lester's hunting dogs bolted to the truck and yowled as we came to a stop. One might think they would be eaten alive if they stepped out of the car at first sight. However, the most these dogs will do is lick ya to death.

My baby cousins ran one by one from the

porch to say hi. Darcy Lynn was standing with her arms crossed on the top step when Aunt Lou came out to see who it was. In the distance, Uncle Lester was by the woodshed, tinkering with something. Daddy went to him while my baby cousins followed mama and carried the presents she'd bought. I hung back and braced myself. I could already hear Darcy Lynn purring as I shuffled across the front yard.

"Robert Lee," she waved. "Oh, Robert Lee!"

I made my way up the steps and greeted her with a nod. "Darcy."

She giggled and grabbed my hand. "Oh, I'm so happy to see you. Come sit with me in the swing for a spell."

"Okay," I mumbled.

Once we were settled, she got as close to me as possible and cooed, "Isn't this time of year so magical?"

"Yep."

I'd pert-near scooted as far as I could as she continued. "So, what have y'all been up to today?"

"Just shopping."

"How nice!"

She glanced around. "Where's that friend of yours, Emmett, is it?"

"He's not with us."

"That's good. It gives us more time together."

I cleared my throat. "You do know he's my boyfriend, Darcy Lynn?"

"Oh," she waved. "That's just a phase you're going through. You just haven't met the right girl yet."

She slid her hand up my thigh, prompting me to jump up and distance myself. She appeared offended, "Where are you going, Robert Lee?"

I held out my hand. "Darcy, I need to be honest with you. You make me very uncomfortable, and I don't like it when you touch me."

She rose and pouted before resting her hands on my chest. "Well, I do declare. You know I mean no harm. I just think a handsome man like you should be with a woman who'll take care of him."

"Darcy, I ain't interested in girls! Do you understand?"

She grabbed my hand and moved it to her breast. "But Robert Lee, I need a man real bad. I got all these urges that need to be taken care of soon, or I'll just burst!"

I tore away from her and ran down the steps with her in tow. "Stop," I yelled.

She paused and looked confused. Before I could continue, Uncle Lester shouted from across the field. "Darcy Lynn! You put that boy down right now. He ain't interested in you. Besides, he's your cousin."

She frowned and stormed back toward the house, then rushed inside. As she did, the door slammed behind her. I let out a sigh of relief as dad yelled, "We're fixing to go hunting, Robert Lee. Why don't you come with us?"

"Thank God," I quipped before running to them. I'd never been so happy to hear my daddy calling for me in my life. Otherwise, I'd have to go back inside and deal with Darcy again. I honestly hope she finds somebody who can handle her one day. For now, I'm just thankful it ain't gonna be me. Why can't she just take no for an answer?

Daddy let out a woodsy laugh as he wrapped his arm around my neck, "Boy, that girl was on you like a hawk on titmouse."

I just sighed as Uncle Lester added, "I ain't gonna say I support your lifestyle Robert Lee, but I will say I certainly understand it."

"That's because Louelle keeps your balls in her purse!"

Uncle Lester punched dad's arm, "Hey, I wear the pants in this family."

"They must be too tight with that gaggle of girls you got for spawn."

I bit my lip to suppress a laugh and attempted to change the subject. "What are we hunting?"

"Squirrels," Lester replied. "Your Aunt Lou is fixin' to make some squirrel gumbo and mountain oysters later."

"Mountain oysters?"

"Pig balls," dad growled.

"Oh, yuck!"

Uncle Lester and Daddy laughed as we started down the trail and disappeared into the woods. Once we'd found a suitable place to hide, daddy and I kept our eyes open and focused on the treetops while Lester watched the ground. We'd been out there for some time when we heard a few shots and someone yell, "Hold your fire, someones been hit."

"What the hell," daddy asked as Lester stood. A young man with another one hanging on to him emerged. One of them was holding his arm. "Who are they?" I asked.

"Some neighbor boys."

He rushed to their aide while daddy and I sat back. "Homer Dave, what the hell are you boys doing out here?"

"We was huntin' deer, but I accidentally shot Jethro Lee."

"Damnit, you two don't need to be out here hunting if you can't tell the difference between a squirrel and your hunting partner."

"I know," Homer said with empathy as Uncle Lester checked the boy's wound.

"You grazed him pretty good. Let's get him to the house and see if Lou can get him bandaged up."

"I'm real sorry about this, Mr. Lester."

"It's fine. Just make sure you be more careful when your out in these woods."

As he helped the boys back to the house, he shouted mine and daddy's direction. "Y'all just go on without me. I'll try to get back after we get ole' Jethro here sewn back up."

"Damn," Daddy growled. "I sure am thankful he's alright."

"Me too," I sighed.

After a few minutes, daddy broke the silence. "After we get a couple of squirrels for your Uncle, I think we'll round up mama and head home. If we don't get back soon, word will travel down the mountain, and we don't want your Emmett to get worried about you."

"Emmett," I whispered.

The thought that he might think I was shot was ripping my heart out. If word gets down the mountain, he'll be worried sick. "Daddy!"

"Yeah?"

"We need to get home soon. If Emmett Ray hears that someone got shot up here, he'll be worried sick."

Just as I explained, Daddy fired a shot and got a fat one nearby on the ground. He turned to me, "Let's get one more, and then we'll go."

I quickly scanned the ground nearby and spotted one not too far from where daddy shot his. I let off a shot and got him. Then, daddy and I rushed to get them before making our way back to the house. As we were walking, I whispered under my breath, "Don't worry, Emmett, I'll be home soon."

PART THREE

EMMETT

Mama's phone rang from the coffee table. I picked it up and rushed it to the kitchen where she was cooking the roast Robert Lee's mom sent yesterday. "Who is it?"

"Some number from Virginia."

"Huh?"

Mom slid up to answer and listened. "Sherri, this is Libby. I just wanted to call and let you know that we won't be home until after dark. We stopped to visit my sister Lou up here in Lee County. While we were visiting, one of the guys got shot out in the woods hunting squirrels. My brother-in-law Lester is taking him to the hospital now."

"What do you mean got shot? Who?"

The phone cut out "... Lee."

"Who," mom shouted. The line went dead.

"W-what is it, mama?"

She covered her mouth with her hands and stared straight ahead before stretching out her arms. "Come here, baby?"

I started to cry, "What? What is it?"

She stroked the back of my head. "The guys

went hunting while they were in Virginia. Apparently, one of them was shot in the woods."

I tore away and shook my head. "No!" I started to back away as she continued. "Honey, I think it's Robert Lee."

I shook my head as the tears began to fall. I ran out of the house and onto the porch. The world was spinning around me. My heartbeat accelerated as mom shouted from inside, "Emmett, come back!"

I bolted down the stairs and towards the barn. Once I was inside, I tried to catch my breath. I spun around in search of a place to sit as memories of making love to him flooded my mind. Finally, I leaned against the wall and slowly slid to the ground as I clutched my chest. A whimper escaped me. Everything I'd come to know. All the love in my heart. All the hope I had in this world was bleeding from my eyes in the form of tears. The boy I intended on spending the rest of my life with was now on the way to the hospital, fighting for his life.

"God," I shouted upward. "Dear God, Why?"

I leaned forward and laid on the ground as sobs escaped my body. Never again would I feel his arms around me. Never again would I feel his lips against mine. Never again would I hear his voice... his laugh... his breath. When I'd cried all the tears I could, I fought my way to my knees and crossed my fingers. It'd been a long time since I prayed, but it was all I could do at this moment. "God, if there is a God. If I can't have Robert Lee, I don't want nothin' at all. No presents. No dinner. No anything until I'm in his arms again. Please... so many people have so much. All I want is him, and I promise I'll never miss the chance to tell him I love him again."

The barn door opened, and mom rushed to me. As she took me in her arms, she kissed the side of my head. "Oh, Emmett Ray, you scared me so much."

I clung to her as I wailed. "Please tell me he's okay, mama. Please tell me he's gonna come down the driveway any second in his daddy's pickup. Mama, please?"

"I would if I could," she whispered. "I would if I could."

Another sob escaped me as I buried my face in her neck. In my ear, I heard her whisper a prayer, "God, we need a miracle here. A Christmas miracle. If you can hear me, bring Robert Lee home safe and save Christmas for my little boy, who loves him more than words can say.

ROBERT LEE

It was nearly eleven at night when we could finally get away from Aunt Lou's. My baby cousins were put to bed long ago. Uncle Lester didn't get back from the hospital with the others until eight. Jethro Lee and Homer were fine after the incident. The doctor managed to patch the boy up with a few stitches, which he proudly showed off to everyone in the house.

Darcy Lynn had finally lost interest in me and taken to Jethro. She patted and massaged his hand while talking about how brave he was the whole time he was here. During all this, daddy and I used our time to clean the squirrels for Aunt Lou. I couldn't help but ask him why Darcy Lynn suddenly took a liking to a boy who she's been around all her life. Daddy just shook his head and declared he didn't know. Then told me just to be thankful she wasn't pining after me anymore.

You should know that a southern goodbye is never easy. It starts with you and your kin standing up and declaring you best be hitting the road. The others then strike up a conversation again about how you shouldn't be a stranger and call if you ever need anything. You edge a little closer to the door, as one of them says, "We need to do this more often." Then, you make promises that you will and continue towards the door.

Now, this time, you may or may not be able to grasp the screen door handle. That depends on how many people you have to hug first. If you do manage to get out the door, the whole family proceeds to follow you to your car, and you commence with a second farewell conversation. This will go on until one of the parties eventually gets too exhausted to trade niceties anymore. Follow that with one more round of hugs; then you're in the car.

But wait, the family whose home you were visiting then have to make sure all children and dogs are out of the way before clearing the path themselves. That's when the waving begins. You continue to wave until no one is in sight. Cue my daddy growling, "Lord have mercy, I thought we would never get out of there."

Mama smiles and looks nostalgic as she replies, "It was a real nice visit, though." As the "kid," I remain silent and keep from expressing any opinions that might be considered rude. However, in my mind, I'm cussing like a sailor and swearing that I'll never endure this again—also, thanking the good Lord that it's over. On the ride home, you're just numb and exhausted. But this time, I was anxious as well. I hope Emmett is okay. I imagine the news has traveled through the mountain grapevine by now, and you can be sure that details were left out.

We finally pulled into our driveway around midnight. Mama fell asleep somewhere along the way, leaving daddy and me to ride in awkward silence back over the mountain. He turned on the radio to a country station playing Christmas songs at one point. Dolly Parton's *Hard Candy Christmas* came on, and I got misty-eyed. I just want to be home, with Emmett, holding him, listening to him prattle on about nothing in particular.

I had no time to waste. Even though it was after midnight, I'd make that drive through the windy Chestnut Knob to see my baby tonight. Daddy helped mama inside as I grabbed Emmett's present and piled into the farm truck. Daddy shouted from the porch as I did, "If you spend the night over there, don't forget to be back for chores. These animals still have to be fed."

"But it's Christmas Eve, Daddy."

He thought for a moment, then forced a smile. "Well, I suppose with the holiday and all you can have today and tomorrow off. But you best be well-rested and ready to work the day after Christmas."

"Yes, sir! Thank you so much, paw!"

"You're welcome," he waved. "Be sure to be over here for dinner tonight and tomorrow."

"Yes, sir."

On that note, I started the truck and raced down the graveled road. Little does Emmett know; I've got one more trick up my sleeve for Christmas. While I was out today, I had the chance to think about many things, and I'd made a decision. There's something important I need to ask him. I just hope he gives me the answer I need to hear.

EMMETT

I'd been lying on the couch all evening waiting for word that Robert Lee was okay. All kinds of bad things go through your mind when you're waiting for potentially bad news. The thought that I'd never love anyone again if Robert Lee was gone crossed my mind. Maybe I'd run away and go back to Indiana. Perhaps I'd just end it all so I could be with him in eternity. I know that they were just passing delusions. Most likely, I'd just stay here and forever mourn the boy I once loved.

I wiped away another tear as lights flashed through the living room window. Mom had gone to bed a while ago. But she left her phone next to me if someone called with news. With squinted eyes, I drew back the curtain and gazed outside. The lights were from a truck that had just pulled up, but I couldn't make out who it was. My heart sank. It was probably his dad here to break the news.

I swallowed hard and attempted to compose myself as I opened the front door. A chill from the night air caught my t-shirt and prompted me to cross my arms. The breeze tousled my hair as the person from the truck slowly approached. My hands folded to my mouth as I recognized the lazy shuffle. I erupted from the front door and down the stairs into the snow. He opened his arms and smiled big as I crashed into him. It didn't even matter that it was cold.

We held for the longest time before I finally managed to pull away and meet his gaze. "B-but how? I thought that you...."

He shook his head. "This is exactly what I was worried about. Emmett Ray, it wasn't me. The boy that got shot was named Jethro Lee. He's a neighbor boy who lives near my Aunt Louelle in Lee County."

I attacked him again and, this time, squeezed even tighter than before. There in the silent night, I could hear his heart beating. I could hear him breathe, and my heart began to beat again. "You don't know all the horrible things that went through my mind," I whimpered.

"I'm here now," he whispered, "and I always will be."

His sentimental tone prompted me to pull

away and meet his gaze again. He leaned in for a kiss as I did, and I willingly accepted and savored his lips like candy. Like the sweetest candy, I'd ever tasted in my life. When he pulled away, he lifted his hand to reveal a gift bag stuffed with pretty tissue. "Got you something."

I sighed and took it, "Just knowing that you're okay is the only present I need."

Robert Lee smirked, "Now, what kind of boyfriend would I be if I didn't get my love a little somethin', somethin' for Christmas."

I grinned and peeked inside. Carefully I lifted the delicately wrapped figurine and gasped. "Oh, Robert Lee, it's beautiful! I absolutely love lighthouses."

"Really?"

"Yes, I do."

He reached toward the bottom and flicked a switch. When he did, the sound of sea birds and waves echoed from a speaker as a tiny light spun between us. It was just enough to cast a glow over our faces as it twirled around. Slowly, our faces moved closer together, and he devoured my lips. I firmly held the lighthouse between us as our tongues spun around in a passionate dance. He knew just how to drive me crazy. He always did.

When we separated, he rested his forehead against mine, "You, what's so special for you about a lighthouse?"

"What?" I whispered.

His voice was low and slow as he answered.

"Lighthouses are a symbol of strength. They are a beacon of hope guiding wayward and lost sailor's home. They can withstand the strongest storms and provide shelter to keep the sea birds warm. They are so much more than just a building. They are a symbol of hope. A guiding light reassuring you that no matter how lost or alone you feel, there's something always there to guide you home."

"That's beautiful."

"Emmett?"

"Yes, Robert Lee?"

"I want to be your lighthouse."

Before I could reply, he shifted and fell to one knee. My hand covered my mouth as he produced a simple wedding band. "I got to thinking about life today. I got to thinking about how much I love you and how I don't want to waste another moment being your boyfriend. Emmett Ray, I want to be your husband. I want to take care of you. I want to give you the best life any boy can. I swear to God if you say yes, I'll be faithful. I'll be true. I'll never have eyes for anyone but you. Just give me a chance.

I shook my head, yes, as tears slid down my cheeks. Slowly he slipped the tiny band on my finger then rose to meet me with another kiss. There in front of my Grandma's old farmhouse, as the snow slowly fell on Christmas Eve, Robert Lee Hawkins asked me to marry him. I said yes. When he pulled away, he exhaled a frosty breath and whispered. "Merry Christmas, Emmett."

I closed my eyes and brushed my nose against

his, "Merry Christmas, Robert Lee."

Quietly, we slipped up the stairs to my room and began getting undressed. I sat the lighthouse with its rotating light on the dresser and fell into Robert Lee's embrace. We stood there naked, exploring one another's bodies with our hands. Warmth and light swirled around us, like the presents beneath a tree.

One kiss led to another, one stolen breath after another. It was everything and more than I could have wished for. Eventually, we found our way onto the bed and merged our bodies just as the ocean waves meet the sand. His body was lapping at mine and mine at his in unbridled passion. Things took a turn as he pinned my hand behind my head and kissed his way down to my wanton cock. It was trembling and waving in the wind as his tongue barely touched it and whirled around the tip and shaft.

I was moaning and whimpering in ecstasy as he teased me to the brink of orgasmic bliss. Finally, my need to be fulfilled was achieved when he slid his warm lips down the shaft and further to the base of my balls. "Oh God, yes," I exhaled as my body squirmed beneath him. It didn't take long with his bobbing to make me moan, "I'm gonna blow."

He pulled away and turned his gaze upward. "Come for me, baby. Give me all of that sweet boy love."

I let out a grunt, followed by a sigh as wave after wave of my load shot out and rained onto my belly. When it was through, Robert Lee pounced and lapped all of it up before coming to meet me in a kiss. It was so hot and kinky to taste my essence on his lips. It was so taboo. I've said it before, and I'll say it again. He knows just what to do to drive me absolutely insane.

SHERRI (EMMETT'S MOM)

I thought I heard something, so I got up to check on Emmett and make him go to bed. 4 A.M. He probably wasn't going to hear anything tonight. As I passed his room, I noticed the bedroom door open and saw him snuggled up next to Robert Lee. My heart danced with joy, but I didn't want to wake them. I could see a lighthouse on the dresser with the light circling the room and sounds of birds and waves echoing throughout.

I placed my hand over my heart and smiled. This year has certainly been full of changes: some good and some bad. At first, I was worried about coming back home and making Emmett leave the life we knew behind. But I see now that it was one of the best decisions I've ever made. In the hallway just outside his room hangs a picture of him, his dad, and me. I lifted my hand to touch the glass and whispered, "Merry Christmas, Darling. I sure wish you were here."

All in all, I must say that this Christmas in the mountains has been one of the best we've ever had so far. I know in time that Emmett and Robert Lee will eventually get a place of their own and move out. I hope they stay close by and don't leave their old mom out here by herself. Now that the only man I ever needed in my life is gone, I need the last one I have more than ever. I took a ragged breath, sniffled, and started back towards my room. "Not tonight," I whispered. "Not tonight." Then, I rubbed away a tear and closed my door behind me once I was inside.

THE END
(for now)

EPILOGUE

EMMETT

Robert Lee and I spent Christmas Eve day sleeping in. We woke up just before noon to the house filled with glorious smells of mom cooking and baking downstairs. When we finally headed down, she greeted Robert Lee with a big hug, "Tell your mama she needs to get a better phone. It cut out right when she was telling us who got shot!"

Robert Lee apologized and explained that it was a neighbor boy who lived nearby his aunt. We were a little scared to tell her about the other present he gave me. However, she found out on her own when she saw the ring on my hand during lunch. Robert Lee apologized and explained that he would have asked for her permission, but the moment was perfect last night.

Mom just smiled and made us promise we wouldn't run off anywhere to get married and that she wanted to be a part of the ceremony and everything. She also offered help to tell his folks if Robert Lee needed any. They've really come around, though, since we met back in the Spring. So, we hope that it will be a celebratory event and not one clouded with drama and ultimatums.

After lunch, we retired to the living room and spent most of the day watching Christmas movies between munching on appetizers. Everything worked out perfectly because we celebrate Christmas on Christmas Eve, and his family celebrates Christmas Day.

Before he left, I gave him his present, a new camouflage outfit, and a knife with a picture of deer on the handle. He loved it. When it came time for us to say goodbye, for now, mama revealed that she got us phones so we could stay in touch. Not just with each other but with her as well. The signal might be spotty, but they do alright here and there.

As we embraced and kissed each other goodnight, he smiled and observed the ring on my hand. "I can't wait until you're mine officially."

"Me too," I sighed as I rested my forehead against his.

After a few more stolen kisses, and one last hug, I stood at the bottom of the porch and waved as his truck disappeared around the bend. With winter truly starting to settle in, I don't know what's to come. But I just know it will be something extraordinary. This was a year full of changes, full of heartbreak, and full of love. Come next year. I can't wait for Spring to return so Robert Lee and I can start planning our wedding. In the meantime, with all of my heart and all of my soul, I wish you and yours a very Happy Holidays and so much more.

-Love Emmett.

ABOUT THE AUTHOR

Daniel Elijah Sanderfer

Daniel Elijah Sanderfer is a best-selling author of over eighty MM and gay romance themed books. He was born in Stuart, Virginia, and raised in Virginia's southside region. He started his work career young, working various jobs as a hotel housekeeper and as a volunteer for his local Salvation Army.

In 2004, he met his husband, William, and moved to Indiana where he resided for fifteen years before moving back to the Blue Ridge Mountain region of Virginia in spring of 2021. He retired from the hospitality industry in 2015 to become a full-time caretaker for his husband who is disabled.

Now, he writes stories to warm the heart that often contain fragments of his life. He believes with all the negativity in the world that stories should be light and evoke his readers to think, hope, and dream of better days. He lives in a very small mountain town and seldom ventures out. He connects with his readers by posting in his Facebook fan group and welcomes anyone who enjoys his work.

Most of his books can be found on Amazon, as well as a limited selection of audiobooks in audible. Please feel free to send him a friend request and join his group, Sanderfer's Socialites

BOOKS IN THIS SERIES

Whiskey Threnody

When Emmett Ray moves to the hills of Tennessee, he never expected to meet the boy of his dreams. Robert Lee is a sandy-blonde hillbilly angel with an accent as thick as the Daniel Boone National Forest. Before Emmett arrived, he wasn't sure what he wanted out of life. Now, he'll stop at nothing to make Emmett his boy.

Whiskey Threnody

When Emmett Ray moves to the hills of Tennessee, he never expected to meet the boy of his dreams. Robert Lee is a sandy-blonde hillbilly angel with an accent as thick as the Daniel Boone National Forest. Before Emmett arrived, he wasn't sure what he wanted out of life. Now, he'll stop at nothing to make Emmett his boy.

However, when his father catches him sneaking back home after curfew, he bans Robert Lee from seeing Emmett ever again. An altercation ensues, prompting Robert Lee to run away, but that's not the end of his troubles. Can two virgin boys on the road to manhood discover what it takes to be together in such a prejudiced atmosphere, or will the love they found be lost forever inside the backwoods of adversity?

Join best-selling author Daniel Elijah Sanderfer for this beautiful lament of adolescence and discover the true meaning of love and family.

Printed in Great Britain
by Amazon

20723550R00037